# WARRIOR HEROES

## THE SAMURAI'S ASSASSIN

First published 2015 by A & C Black
An imprint of Bloomsbury Publishing Plc
50 Bedford Square, London WC1B 3DP

www.bloomsbury.com

Bloomsbury is a registered trademark of Bloomsbury Publishing Plc

ISBN 978-1-4729-0466-9

A CIP catalogue for this book is available from the British Library.

Printed and bound by CPI Group (UK) Ltd, Croydon CR0 4YY

1 3 5 7 9 10 8 6 4 2

# WARRIOR HEROES

## THE SAMURAI'S ASSASSIN

### BENJAMIN HULME-CROSS

Illustrated by
**Angelo Rinaldi**

A & C BLACK
AN IMPRINT OF BLOOMSBURY
LONDON  NEW DELHI  NEW YORK  SYDNEY

# CONTENTS

## INTRODUCTION
## THE HALL OF HEROES

The Hall of Heroes is a museum
all about warriors throughout
history. It's full of swords, bows
and arrows, helmets, boats, armour,
shields, spears, axes and just
about anything else that a warrior
might need. But this isn't just
another museum full of old stuff
in glass cases - it's also haunted
by the ghosts of the warriors whose
belongings are there. Our great
grandfather, Professor Blade, set
up the museum and when he died he
started haunting the place too. He
felt guilty about the trapped ghost
warriors and vowed he would not
rest in peace until all the other
ghosts were laid to rest first. And
that's where Arthur and I come in…

On the night of the Professor's funeral Arthur and I broke into the museum - we knew it was wrong but we just couldn't help ourselves. And that's when we discovered something very weird. When we are touched by one of the ghost warriors we get transported to the time and place where the ghost lived and died. And we can't get back until we've fixed whatever it is that keeps the ghost from resting in peace. So we go from one mission to the next, recovering lost swords, avenging deaths, saving loved ones or doing whatever else the ghost warrior needs us to do.

Fortunately while the Professor was alive I wrote down everything he ever told us about these warriors in a book I call *Warrior Heroes* -

so luckily we do have some idea of
what we're getting into each time
- even if Arthur does still call
me 'Finn the geek'. But we need
more than a book to survive each
adventure because wherever we go
we're surrounded by war and battle
and the fiercest fighters who ever
lived, as you're about to find out!

# CHAPTER 1

Finn drifted lazily towards consciousness, dreaming that he was leaping to impossible heights and then rushing back down to earth, only to leap even higher into the air once more. He licked his lips and tasted brine, noting that heavy rain was pelting his back as he took another giant leap skywards. It was just as he reached the highest point of the arc and hung there for a moment, waiting for the fall that he woke with a jolt.

A huge wave rolled forward and Finn swooped down the back of it, slipping off a plank of wood that he had been half-lying on and gulping down a mouthful of sea water as he shouted out in panic. Spluttering, he kicked and hoisted himself back onto the tiny float, at the same time trying to blink and shake the water out of his eyes before the next wave began to lift him up again. As he reached the top of the wave he twisted around, praying he would see some way out of this nightmare that he had swapped for the Professor's study. He felt marginally better when he saw that the waves were surging towards land and that he was in the middle of a small bay.

Finn pulled himself further forward on the plank, as if he were lying on a surfboard, and as he rose with the next wave he pushed himself up on his arms to get a better view. He could see very little of the shoreline through the torrent of rain, but what he did see turned his stomach and the feeling of relief he had felt just moments ago quickly evaporated. The huge rollers were breaking over a line of jagged rocks that stuck up out of the sea like teeth, and he was heading straight for them.

Struggling against the powerful current, Finn slid the plank around, away from the jagged rocks. He began kicking towards the open sea, but for every small bit of progress he made, the next wave carried him back towards the shore. Shaking with fear, Finn turned again to face the rocks. All he could do was hope that a wave carried him over the top instead of smashing him to pieces against the vicious-looking spikes. There was one spot where the gap between the tips of the rocks seemed to be wide enough that he might just get through, but he had no idea what lay beneath the water. Using what little energy he had left, Finn turned side-on to the waves and tried to line up with the gap as the rocks grew closer and bigger.

Three more waves and he would be on them. The first wave drew him forward and then rolled past, crashing violently against the rocks. The second wave pushed him on and then sucked him unexpectedly to the side so that he was barely in line with the gap any more. Frantically he tried to shimmy back to his original position, and then the third wave picked him up and began to curl over him. He kicked forward, his whole body taut as he gripped the plank with all his might. The wave surged and began to break. Finn tried to block out the sight of the rocks to either side of him as he accelerated with the wave and began to hurtle down towards the foaming, flatter water below. As he hit the foam his plank was torn from his grasp and he had a split second to catch a lungful of air before the wave swallowed him and tumbled him over and over in dizzying somersaults.

He felt something against his feet and kicked down onto sand before he was upended by the next churning wave. The next time his feet hit the ground he staggered forward, still up to his chest in the frothing surf. He heard a shout and then a coil of rope splashed into the sea in front of him. Finn leapt towards it and grabbed hold just as the next wave ripped him off his feet again and sent him spinning. Suddenly the rope was being pulled back and Finn floated on the water, breathing in huge gulps of air, holding tight and letting the waves wash over him as he was reeled in towards the beach.

He staggered out of the water and collapsed coughing onto the sand, seawater streaming from his nose and mouth. As he rolled over and looked up through sheets of pouring rain, he found himself staring into the concerned faces of a boy and a girl, and wondered for the first time where he was.

"You must come with us," said the boy, bowing at the same time. "The typhoon is getting worse. We saw the ship sink and you are very lucky to survive. Welcome to Japan."

"Thank you," Finn began. "But my brother..."

"There are no more people in the sea. We can talk later," said the girl, also bowing. "First you must come with us out of the rain."

They helped Finn to his feet and each holding one of his arms they began to lead him away from the beach towards a line of trees. He had never felt so wet in his life. The hot, heavy air pushed and sucked rain in all directions. This was rain he'd never experienced before. It was a challenge to even breathe without inhaling water.

He always felt disorientated at first after

travelling back in time, but as the adrenalin rush brought on by his narrow escape began to subside, Finn cast his mind back to the Professor's study...

\* \* \*

"So boys, what can you tell me about the samurai?" It seemed to Finn that there was something unusual in the Professor's tone as he paced around the study. Something like sadness.

"Total psychopaths!" Arthur exclaimed. "Amazing swordsmen who could take on huge numbers of ordinary men all by themselves and kill all of them. Oh, and ritual suicide - seppuku. They'd slit their own bellies open rather than face dishonour."

The Professor considered Arthur for a moment and then remarked, "The greatest samurai swordsmen in medieval Japan went their whole lives without ever killing anyone."

"What?" said Arthur, frowning. "How could they have been great warriors if they never fought?"

Finn smiled to himself. Arthur was always so hot-headed. The idea of a warrior fighting and winning without killing must have seemed ridiculous to him.

"They believed that defeating an opponent was about winning a mental battle," the Professor explained. "Dissuade him from fighting by convincing him he would lose. And if you do start fighting, convince him he is going to lose and force his surrender. But that wouldn't make for enough action in one of your Samurai movies, eh Arthur?"

"Self-control," Finn joined in. "Weren't the samurai all about self-control and discipline?"

"That's right old chap," said the Professor. "The best samurai were completely in control of their minds, bodies and emotions. Mind you," he went on. "Not all of them reached such high standards. But the best of them were finer warriors than have been seen anywhere else in the world."

There it was again, thought Finn. The Professor seemed sad. No, not sad... nostalgic.

"The man you are about to meet was a truly great samurai. Hanzo Uchida, a swordsman of exquisite skill that he very rarely used. If ever there were a warrior who deserved to rest in peace it is this man..."

The Professor trailed off and Finn caught Arthur's eye. There was definitely something weird in the way the Professor was talking about this warrior ghost. But before either boy could ask any questions they both noticed the atmospheric changes that always preceded a ghost's entrance. The air cooled rapidly and seemed to grow stiller just as the lights in the study cut out abruptly and the group were plunged into darkness.

The boys peered through the blackness and waited for the sound of footsteps, or the study door creaking open. But nothing came.

"Old friend," said the Professor. "How often I have thought of you."

"He's not here yet," Arthur hissed, and then drew in his breath as the Professor lit a candle and a shadowy form stepped silently forward into the thin circle of light. He wore loose cotton trousers and a kimono jacket that was strapped tightly around the waist. His whole torso was stained red with blood.

"Many years have passed, Blade," said the samurai softly. "And now you may be able to help me."

"It would be an honour, Hanzo Uchida," replied the Professor, "Though it will be the boys here who do the work."

Hanzo Uchida looked intently at the two boys and bowed to each in turn. "A man lives on through his descendants," he said. "And I see that these boys carry your spirit." There was something in Hanzo Uchida's eyes that Finn had never seen before. They were perfectly still, perfectly focussed.

"How can we help?" Finn asked, entranced.

"It is very simple." Hanzo Uchida replied. "I allowed myself to be killed by a tyrant in the hope that he would spare the others who lived in the area. The tyrant's name was Kenji Kuroda."

"Let me guess," said Arthur. "He didn't spare them?

"At first yes, but a few days later he massacred them all," said Hanzo Uchida evenly. "Because my son Tatsushi tried to kill him." The samurai's eyes seemed to cloud over for a fraction of a second before their clarity was back. "The boy wanted to avenge my death but he acted rashly. Not with the restraint that befits a samurai."

"So you want us to stop your son avenging your death?" Arthur seemed confused.

"Not necessarily," Hanzo Uchida stared at

Arthur intently. "You must ensure that the boy thinks before he acts. He must think about the lives of the other villagers. And if he wishes to avenge my death he must do so in a careful way that may succeed, not in a blood-rage." Arthur swallowed nervously as Hanzo Uchida continued steadily. "I can see that the two of you together embody instinct and caution. Work together and guide my son."

Before Finn could ask the Professor why he had called the samurai an old friend, Hanzo Uchida stepped silently forward and placed a hand lightly on each boy's shoulder. The air in the room seemed to circle around them, faster and faster, until the study had vanished and the boys were spinning through darkness towards a sound like that of violent waves crashing against rocks.

# CHAPTER 2

Finn gasped with relief as he staggered into the wooden building and collapsed to the floor. After the beating the ocean had dealt him, and the deluge of rain, the cool, dry room felt like paradise. His delight increased further when his rescuers slid back a screen to reveal his brother sitting comfortably on the floor and eating what seemed to be a large ball of rice with his hands.

"Knew they'd find you!" spluttered Arthur cheerfully through a mouthful of rice. "Come and get some food. It's simple stuff but really hits the spot. Tatsushi! Mayuko! You are both heroes!"

"How did you get here?" Finn asked, slightly irritated by his brother's chirpy state.

"Swam," said Arthur, looking over Finn's shoulder at their hosts and then back to Finn with his eyebrows raised. Finn kicked himself. They always had to be careful what they said about how they arrived in a new place. They couldn't end up having to explain that time travel was involved.

"I fear there are no other survivors," said the boy. "My sister Mayuko saw the ship go down a few hours ago and we thought nobody could have survived – it sank so quickly. But you boys are here. You are brave and fortunate and you will be welcome at my father's house for as long as you need to stay."

Finn closed his eyes for a moment. It was desperately sad to think that if these were Hanzo Uchida's children, and it seemed almost certain that they were, then at some point soon their lives were going to fall apart.

"You are very kind," said Finn. "I hope that we can find a way to repay you for what you have done today."

Tatsushi bowed his head slightly, turned away and slipped into a whispered conversation with his sister. Finn studied the pair while Arthur went back to his rice. It was impossible to guess their age, except to say that they seemed older than Arthur but not yet adult. Both wore simple kimonos and had jet-black hair. Tatsushi was no taller than Arthur but his broad frame indicated great strength. His sister had slightly paler skin and softer eyes, and although she had said very little, Finn got the impression that she made the decisions – Tatsushi did most of the talking but he often glanced at her before speaking. It was very difficult to imagine these quiet, controlled people losing their cool, whatever the provocation.

"Excuse me," said Mayuko, "May we ask your names?"

"Blade," said Arthur, jabbing a finger in Finn's direction. "He's Finn. I'm Arthur."

"Blade!" Tatsushi exclaimed, his eyes widening. "Do you know my father's friend, the great warrior William Blade?"

"He's our..." Finn trailed off, remembering how the Professor and Hanzo Uchida had spoken to each other. "We are related, yes."

"Then you will be even more welcome at my father's house!" cried Tatsushi, hopping around excitedly. "Come, Mayuko, let's find the Blades some clothes and we can get back to father."

Once their rescuers had left the room Finn turned to Arthur and whispered, "There's only one way they could know the Professor..."

"He must have been here himself." Arthur finished the thought.

The boys sat in silence, pondering this new twist on their adventure. They had always believed that they were unique in their ghost-driven time travel. Now it seemed they were not alone. But if the Professor had been here before and somehow helped Hanzo Uchida, what did that mean for their mission? Before they could explore the possibilities, Tatsushi reappeared, sliding the screen closed behind him and presenting them each with a neat pile of clothes to replace the torn, sodden rags that the ocean had left plastered to their skin.

They slipped into the loose, cotton trousers and kimono-style jackets, fumbling in their attempts to fasten the unfamiliar belts. Tatsushi stepped forward and wrapped the fabric around their waists for them.

"My father says that William Blade was the same," said Tatsushi, laughing. "When he came here he too found everything very strange. But people found him strange also – nobody had ever seen a man from outside of Japan before. He was so tall, and had such a big face! People wanted to turn him away but luckily my father is a very wise man and – "

"We should go," called Mayuko through the screen, cutting Tatsushi off mid-sentence. "Are you ready?"

The oppressive rain still bore down outside and Mayuko handed around wooden-framed umbrellas as they stepped out of the hut and began walking further inland.

"So how did William Blade come to be friends with your father?" Finn asked as they climbed steadily through the trees to higher ground.

Tatsushi explained that many years ago William washed up ashore from a wreck just as the boys had done, and was rescued by their father who was on his way with a small group of samurai to join an army being mustered to help their overlord, Lord Kuruyama, fight a rival lord. William had accompanied them and had been met with great suspicion by almost everyone, but had eventually won them around and helped them to win a great victory.

"What was the rival Lord's name?" Arthur asked.

"Yosuke Kuroda," Tatsushi replied with a deep frown. "He was killed in battle, but now all these years later his son, Kenji Kuroda, is preparing an army."

"My father says that if Kenji Kuroda and his family grow too strong then we will all suffer greatly," said Mayuko softly.

"Are you afraid?" asked Finn.

"We are not afraid of him," she replied. "But we

do not wish people to suffer and we will do what must be done."

Looking at the softly-spoken girl Finn found himself gazing into dark, still eyes. Just like Hanzo Uchida, he thought sadly.

"Some people might be angry with Kenji Kuroda," Finn commented. "For preparing an army and trying to seize power. But you don't seem angry."

"The true samurai controls their emotions. This is what our father has taught us. Anger is weakness. Cruelty is weakness. Strength is preparing your mind and body so that you can see what needs to be done and can do it properly."

Both Finn and Arthur found themselves profoundly struck by the girl's words and they continued in silence for a while, thinking carefully about what she had said. The trees had disappeared now and the rain had stopped. They were walking along a road with fields on either side, and some distance away they could see a cluster of houses. Tatsushi began urging them on, delighted all over again at the prospect of introducing his new friends to his father.

"My father will be so happy – " the cheerful words died on his lips as suddenly a scream filled the air and flames erupted from the roof of one of the houses in front of them.

Instantly Tatsushi and Mayuko began sprinting towards the village and the boys followed behind quickly, grimly aware of the devastating events that were likely to play out

before them. As they reached the burning house
they saw that the village was larger than it had
first appeared, stretching out before them with
thirty or so buildings on either side of the road.
A wailing crowd had gathered in a circle in the
middle of the village, surrounded by a band of

fierce looking samurai, mounted on horseback, brandishing spears at anyone who tried to break away. Every now and then a fresh scream cut through the wailing and Finn's stomach turned as he thought of what they might be about to witness.

"Mayuko! Tatsushi!" Finn shouted. "We should stay back. This is not a fight we can win." But as he spoke most of the mounted samurai turned and began riding through the village in the opposite direction.

Ignoring Finn's warning, Mayuko and Tatsushi ran forwards towards the crowd and Arthur and Finn had no choice but to follow closely behind. Some of the crowd turned as the runners approached, and seeing Tatsushi and Mayuko they tried to block their way. But Tatsushi and Mayuko ran at such speed that people were knocked out of the way as they carved a path through the villagers and burst through into the open space that the crowd had been circling. Face down in the mud lay a simply-dressed samurai, his long hair streaking out into a growing pool of blood.

"Father!" Mayuko cried, falling to her knees and clutching at her father's back. An anguished scream burst from her chest as she realised that Hanzo Uchida was dead, and Finn found himself fighting back tears as he looked over at Tatsushi, who stood completely motionless, staring down at his father's body with fury in his eyes.

And then things got worse. One of the few marauding samurai who had remained in the village opened up a path through the crowd with his horse and came to a stop beside Mayuko.

"Your father?" he said, grabbing her by the arm and hauling her roughly up onto the horse before she had a chance to respond. "Then you will come with me."

"Mayuko!" Tatsushi screamed, running forward in sudden desperation.

Mayuko looked at her brother and shook her head almost imperceptibly. Tatsushi stopped in his tracks and the mounted samurai grinned down at him with a malicious glint in his eyes.

"Remember!" he shouted, turning away from Tatsushi and addressing the rest of the crowd. "You are all alive because Kenji Kuroda and Hanzo Uchida made a deal. Hanzo Uchida was permitted to take his own life to spare yours but if you resist us in any way we will return and destroy you. Your lives belong to us now, do I make myself clear?"

Nobody spoke. The rider turned his horse around and kicked it into a gallop, while Mayuko hung on. The samurai and Mayuko disappeared around a bend in the road, leaving Tatsushi to his grief, and Finn and Arthur to figure out how they would be able to control Tatsushi's urge for revenge now that not only did his father lie dead in the mud, but his sister had been kidnapped right before his eyes.

EXTRACT FROM *WARRIOR HEROES*
BY FINN BLADE

## SEPPUKU

Seppuku is a ritual suicide.
Sometimes called hara-kiri, this is
something that you wouldn't wish on
your worst enemy.

If you are a samurai then seppuku
is a very specific way of killing
yourself without dishonour. You sit
down in front of a crowd, take a
dagger, grit your teeth and cut your
own belly open. Sounds too horrible
to be true. If it hurts too much the
samurai has someone standing behind
them ready to chop off their head
and put them out of their misery.

## WHY WOULD YOU DO IT?

• If you are on the losing side
  of a battle you might do it to

avoid being captured (and probably tortured).

- If you have been disgraced for any reason you might do it to restore your honour, and protect the rest of your family from dishonour. The idea is that anyone capable of sacrificing themselves in this way has all of their sins wiped clean.

- As a protest against a Lord who you think is wrong about something.

- As the ultimate show of loyalty to your Lord when he dies.

One explanation for the way Japanese soldiers treated captured enemy soldiers so horribly during World War Two is that they couldn't respect enemies who had allowed themselves to be captured rather than committing suicide.

# CHAPTER 3

As night fell it was a desolate party that sat on the bamboo matting of the Uchida family house. Tatsushi had barely uttered a word since the afternoon's horrors, and the other villagers had given Finn and Arthur a wide berth with the exception of a kind old man who bowed and introduced himself as Ryu, Hanzo Uchida's servant. From him the boys had learned that Tatsushi and Mayuko were now orphans – their mother had died giving birth to Mayuko. The boys had tried to engage Ryu and Tatsushi with suggestions about how they might go about recovering Mayuko, but Tatsushi was too consumed with rage to listen, and Ryu also seemed to be suffering with the news of his master's death.

It was only when a group of men from the village arrived at the house that evening that Tatsushi emerged from his shock and rage. The leader of the group stepped forward and bowed.

"We have spoken with every family in the village and are all in agreement. If you wish Tatsushi then we would be honoured to follow you in pursuit of Kenji Kuroda. He and his men have committed a terrible crime and forced a good man to die. They cannot be allowed to get away with it."

"And what of the threat to return and wipe us out if we resist?" said Ryu.

"What of it? We do not wish to live in fear of the Kurodas. We must resist."

"I promise you this," Tatsushi growled. "I will kill that man the moment I next lay eyes on him." The men nodded as Tatsushi spoke. "And you are most welcome to join me."

Finn glanced at Arthur, and then around at the group of villagers. They did not seem like warriors who could take on a band of strong and fierce samurai. In fact things seemed to be heading in the direction that Hanzo Uchida had warned against – an ill-considered, furious attempt at revenge that would inevitably fail.

Finn knew he had to try and steer the group away from this course.

"May I say something?" Finn cleared his throat and Tatsushi nodded. "If all the best men in the village go with you and you fail to kill Kuroda, the village will be defenceless."

"Go on," said Ryu, watching him intently.

All eyes were on Finn as he continued, "If you were to assemble a small group of loyal samurai from outside the village instead, there would be several benefits. First these men could remain here to defend the village should Kuroda return. Second if your group of samurai does find and fight Kuroda they may not be recognised and Kuroda may not retaliate by attacking the village should he defeat us. And third a small group with a mission to kill Kuroda and rescue Mayuko may have a better chance of success than a large group attacking his men head on. One man is easier to defeat than an army."

"I am not afraid of Kuroda's men!" Tatsushi spat. "I'll kill them all!"

"Master," said Ryu gently. "Nobody doubts your courage, but the boy speaks sense. What is it that you want to achieve?"

"Revenge!" cried Tatsushi.

"Then control your emotions!" Ryu snapped. "What use is revenge? Why did your father choose to die? Because he wanted to protect the people of this village. Now, think again. Why do you want Kuroda dead?"

Tatsushi rubbed the back of his head and sighed. "I too want our people to be safe.

We are not safe as long as Kuroda lives. And my sister..." here Tatsushi's red eyes began to fill with tears again.

"We will find her," said Finn. "But that is why you must try to forget about revenge. Think about your goal and put your emotions to one side."

Tatsushi stared around the group for a long moment, then nodded his head.

"My friend is right," he said. "You men should stay here and plan our defences in case the village is attacked again. Ryu, you must get word to Lord Kuruyama and tell him what has happened. It may be that once again the Kurodas are preparing to take on Lord Kuruyama and destroy him, just as they did when my father fought against them.

*With the Professor at his side,* thought Finn.

"I will set off at once," said Ryu, bowing and leaving the room. The other men of the village followed until only the three boys remained.

Finn gazed around the room as he had done so many times that day. The earthy smell of bamboo matting filled the warm air and the paper lanterns Ryu had lit as night fell cast a soft, warm light over the dark wooden walls. An open screen door let in the tinkling sound of water from the garden and everything about the place was so peaceful that once again Finn wondered how these people could be warriors.

"My father never searched for a fight," said Tatsushi, noticing Finn's puzzled expression as he studied the peaceful environment. "He lived in peace but was always prepared for combat if it should find him. Come, let me show you."

He led the brothers across the hallway and into a small room at the centre of the house, and as they stepped across the threshold it was like entering a different world. Arthur's jaw dropped. The weapons that lined the walls were beautifully crafted, elegant and looked exquisitely dangerous. Long spears with slim wooden shafts adorned with pretty ribbons were topped by razor-sharp slicing blades and thrusting points. Ornately carved, well-oiled bows stood waiting to be strung in one corner of the room. Four crested helmets with hideous face masks grimaced insanely back at them from a shelf, beneath which were piled various pieces of deep-red armour. But for all the fascination that these items held, they were but minor distractions from the main focus of the room. On a simple table against a blank wall a sword was cradled by two small wooden props, its gentle, perfect curve a thing of supreme beauty.

"My father's," Tatsushi murmured, lifting it off the props and sliding it out of its lacquered sheath so that it gleamed in the light of the lanterns. "This is the sword that will kill Kenji Kuroda."

The reverent silence that followed these words was broken by the sound of footsteps outside.

"Tatsushi," it was the voice of Ryu, the old man. "Tatsushi are you still here?"

"In here," the boy called and Ryu entered the armoury.

"I have some very important news – very bad news," the old man began, pausing for a moment as he noticed the sword in Tatsushi's hand. "I did not reach Castle Kuruyama. I met some of Lord Kuruyama's servants on the road. The Kurodas have already struck and Lord Kuruyama is dead - poisoned." Finn looked from Ryu to Tatsushi and saw the blood draining from his new friend's face all over again.

"Kenji Kuroda was a guest in the castle and has taken it over from within," Ryu went on, rubbing a hand over his brow. "The servants I met on the road told me that they overheard him plotting - he has dispatched a band of samurai to kill the most dangerous warriors loyal to Lord Kuruyama - those were the samurai who came for your father today but Kenji Kuroda was not among them. When he has killed the samurai he most fears, Kuroda will announce himself as the new Lord."

Tatsushi nodded, teeth clenched. "Then Finn was right - fighting a pitched battle with the samurai would have been pointless. We might have rescued Mayuko but Kuroda would have sent his men back to the village and killed us all."

"So what are we going to do?" asked Arthur.

Tatsushi looked around the room at his companions in turn, then down at his father's sword still resting in his hand.

"We will do everything by stealth," he said. "First we will pursue Kuroda's samurai. If they are looking for men loyal to Lord Kuruyama then we know the villages they will be heading for. We will free Mayuko without revealing ourselves and then head to Castle Kuruyama, where we will find a way of killing Kenji Kuroda."

"But if we free Mayuko – "

"Then eventually Kuroda's men will come back to this village," Tatsushi finished the thought.

"And kill everyone. I have thought of this. But for now they have their mission to kill those loyal to Lord Kuruyama and they won't waste time on us as long as there are still samurai living who remain loyal to him."

"I must warn those who Kuroda will be targeting," said Ryu. "Then the Kuroda gang will take longer to find them and there will be some men left to rise up and make sure that if Kenji Kuroda dies he is replaced by someone we can trust."

Tatsushi nodded, and the two swiftly listed the men whom the Kuroda gang were likely to be searching for. Ryu refused the offer of a weapon to take with him on his quest to find the men, saying that he would arouse less suspicion if he remained unarmed.

"I too remember William Blade," he said to Finn and Arthur. "He fought alongside Master Hanzo Uchida and helped Lord Kuruyama defeat an army raised by Kenji Kuroda's father. He was a very brave man. I hope that you can help us now, just as he did then. And Tatsushi," he said, putting an arm around the boy's shoulders. "Your father has taught you all the skills that you will need. It will not be easy to reach Kenji Kuroda now that he is in the castle, but you can do it. And your chances will be even better with Mayuko at your side. Find Mayuko and the four of you will not fail."

EXTRACT FROM *WARRIOR HEROES*
BY FINN BLADE


## SAMURAI WEAPONS

SWORD

The standard samurai sword has a
blade that is just over two feet
long. It is curved and so is
naturally suited to slicing, though
thrusting is still possible as the
tip is usually pointed. It is made
of steel and is much lighter than
European swords, making it easy to
carry and to handle in battle. It
is of more use in a duel than from
horseback in a battle, but every
samurai has a sword. In fact they
have two, because they also keep a
second, shorter sword, tucked into
their waistband.

## SPEAR

As the samurai ride horses into battle, spears are very important. From horseback a long spear means you can reach your enemy on the ground, and from the ground a long spear means you have a chance of knocking a samurai off his horse. The steel tip can be up to three feet in length, and looks more like a sword than a spear-head.

## BOW

The Japanese bow, or yumi, is quite unusual. It is over two metres in length so has a very long range. It is incredibly strong as it is made from strips of wood and leather, laminated together. The grip is not in the middle, but about two thirds of the way down the bow so that the bottom is much shorter than the top, which makes it easier to use on horseback.

## KUSARI-FUNDO

This is one of many types of
chain weapons used by the samurai.
The simplest are four-foot lengths
of chain with weights at each end.
They can be used to entangle your
opponent's weapon, allowing you
to leap forward and strike with a
second weapon, or else you can use
the weight on one of the ends of the
chain to crush your enemy's skull.

# CHAPTER 4

The three boys walked through the night in silence. Ryu had headed on horseback in a different direction, hoping to overtake the Kuroda gang and forewarn a string of villages that they were likely targets. Tatsushi, Arthur and Finn, meanwhile, were making their way to the village where they thought their enemies were spending the night and where they hoped they would find Mayuko. The air had cooled, and the heavy atmosphere of the previous day's storms had lifted completely.

"Tomorrow it will be autumn," said Tatsushi at one point, and Finn laughed. Everything seemed so clear-cut in medieval Japan. One day summer storms, the next day autumn. "It's good," Tatsushi went on, puzzled by Finn's laughter. "The typhoon has passed. We may be able to travel by boat."

Finn stopped laughing. The idea of getting back into the ocean did not appeal to him, and a glance at his brother told Finn that Arthur felt the same.

"Why would we want to travel by boat?" Arthur asked, a nervous quaver clearly audible in his voice. "I thought we were going to the next village."

"Don't worry brothers," Tatsushi replied. "I do not mean the open sea. There is a narrow inlet that we can cross by boat. It will save us several hours of walking. We won't be on the water for long, and we won't be on it at all if the sea is not calm."

There seemed little point in arguing, and the boys followed Tatsushi off the road and down a muddy, tree-lined track until they saw flashes of moonlight dancing on the black sea.

"We can cross," said Tatsushi curtly when they reached the shore. There was a cool breeze blowing in off the water, which was choppy but nothing like the heaving, churning mass that had nearly drowned them the day before. Looking out they could see lights on the other side of the inlet, and though it was difficult to gauge the distance, it certainly did not seem far.

"Follow me," Tatsushi instructed, and he stepped into the water and began wading along the shore until his path was blocked by a tree that thrust out across the water almost horizontally. The boys followed Tatsushi into the water and it was only when Tatsushi began fiddling with a rope that the boys saw a small wooden boat moored to the other side of the tree.

"How many secret boats do you have?" Arthur asked, impressed.

"Only this one. Mayuko and I made it one summer when we were younger." Tatsushi's voice faltered slightly as he said his sister's name. "We used to play in it and she said we should hide it here. I never thought I would need it for anything important..."

"We will find her, you know," Arthur reassured, resting a hand on Tatsushi's shoulder.

"Yes we will," said Tatsushi, and something about the intensity of his voice frightened Finn. He was beginning to see the fire beneath Tatsushi's calm exterior, and the idea of it erupting did not seem so unlikely after all.

They climbed into the boat and Tatsushi began to paddle them across the narrow strip of water, heading for one of the lights on the other side of the inlet that they had seen earlier.

"We need a story," said Tatsushi suddenly, breaking the silence of the still night air. "My father used to calm me down with stories if I ever needed to be distracted. I will tell you about

Akira, the samurai who vanished. Akira was the most respected of Lord Kuruyama's samurai. My father always said that he strived every day to be like him. He was a master of all forms of fighting, both in battle and in individual combat. He never displayed anger. He never even raised his voice. In Lord Kuruyama's service he won great honour as a warrior but also as a peacemaker. He had attained perfection as a samurai and many people even suggested that one day he might become Lord of the region, for Kuruyama had no sons of his own.

"Then the great traitor, Yosuke Kuroda, raised his army against Lord Kuruyama. A great battle was fought – William Blade was there and my father too, but the hero of the day was Akira. They say that he tore through Yosuke Kuroda's men like a typhoon. Everyone knew of Akira's bravery – and they were grateful to him for saving them from Yosuke Kuroda's cruelty. Then, a few weeks after the battle, Akira was training a group of young samurai at Castle Kuruyama. He told them that they were to pretend he was an assassin and chase him down as he attempted to break into the castle. He began climbing up the castle walls and ten young samurai chased him. They saw him climb all the way to the top. Seconds later they too climbed onto the roof, but when they got there, he had vanished. After that day he was never seen again."

Arthur and Finn had been listening so intently that they had almost forgotten where they were. Even Tatsushi seemed surprised when he turned his head and saw how close they were to the shore.

As they paddled even closer he stared hard at the black rocks they were approaching, looking for a place to make land. Without warning Tatsushi leapt into the water and began pulling the boat towards a tiny patch of sand.

With Tatsushi still focused on pulling the boat along, Arthur turned to Finn and whispered, "How are we supposed to control his temper? He's in some weird zone the whole time."

"He saw his father murdered less than twelve hours ago. We stick with him. He knows what he has to do – we just have to remind him if he's about to lose it. Anyway, he might calm down a bit if we can get Mayuko back." The boat hissed to a stop as the bottom touched sand and the boys jumped out and helped Tatsushi drag it up out of the water.

"We'll be there in ten minutes," said Tatsushi. "Follow me." And he began scrambling up the rocks and into the darkness of the trees that cloaked the shoreline. After some steep climbing they reached a ridge and Finn stopped to catch his breath. Tatsushi pressed forward immediately, increasing the pace and darting nimbly through the forest, leaping between tree roots and rocks. It was only when Arthur tripped and fell with a curse that Tatsushi looked back. He paused barely long enough for the boys to catch up with him, twitching restlessly as he waited.

"Slow down," Arthur hissed. "If we're so close then we need to be quiet. You make much less noise than us!" This was true. For all Tatsushi's haste he had barely made a sound as he danced along. He nodded, his face taut, and proceeded in a little less of a frenzy but Arthur and Finn still struggled to keep up. When he stopped abruptly, the boys could hear that the night air carried the faint sound of shouts and laughter.

"That is the place," he said. "That is where Mayuko will be, I know it." And he began to walk forwards again.

"Wait," said Finn. "If she is there with Kenji Kuroda's gang then we need a plan if we are going to succeed in freeing her." They had barely spoken about what they would do when they arrived here, and now Finn worried that Tatsushi would be too highly strung to think clearly.

"It is very simple – we will go from house to house until we find her. If anyone tries to stop us, we kill them." Tatsushi replied curtly.

"As soon as one of us draws a sword we may as

well be dead, and Mayuko too. We need a story. What do we say if we are seen?" said Finn.

The boys paused for a moment – unsure of how to take their plan any further.

"I have an idea," said Arthur. "Is this village like yours Tatsushi? With two rows of houses opposite each other?" Tatsushi nodded and Finn prayed that his brother had something that would keep their friend in check.

"This is what we should do. Tatsushi, you should wait just outside the village. Then if we get into any trouble there is still one person left to try and free Mayuko. And anyway, they might recognise you but they have never seen us. Finn and I take one row of houses each. We go from the back of one house to the back of the next until we see or hear something that tells us the Kurodas are here. If we are seen we can say we just washed up ashore after the shipwreck. Then we come back to you Tatsushi when we have some idea of what's going on in the village and where Mayuko might be."

Tatsushi seemed about to object, but then his expression changed completely. "Wait, Mayuko and I used to practise bird calls when we were younger. I can make a call that sounds like the cry of a heron. There is a chance she will know it is me and hopefully she will be able to give us some sign that will lead us to her – with any luck we won't have to search every house in the village at all."

"Good." Arthur nodded. "But if we hear nothing back from Mayuko and we still need to search the village then you must let us do the searching. When the time comes to free her you'll be right there at the front again."

The plan agreed, they crept on downhill as quietly as they could until the trees began to clear and they saw the first lanterns of the village a short way ahead. Tatsushi stopped and cupped his hands to his mouth, letting out three long, harsh screeches. The boys listened intently for a reply, but all they could hear was the raucous laughter of drunk men. Tatsushi tried again, and again they listened. Nothing.

"Arthur," Finn whispered, as Tatsushi desperately tried his call once more, "We leave our swords here. Bows and daggers we can explain. Samurai swords we can't."

Arthur nodded, laying his sword on the

ground next to Finn's. "Tatsushi, keep your bow at the ready but don't shoot unless we're going to be killed. If we get caught it's better they don't know you are here."

"And remember, keep..." Finn paused and frowned. Tatsushi's face was a picture of excitement. Drifting through the air, above and below the noise of the revellers, there floated the faint sound of a girl singing.

"That's her!" Tatsushi exclaimed. He put his head back and gave the heron's cry again. "She's here and we can find her. Come on!"

"It would still be safer if one of us stayed back," Arthur cautioned. "Finn, you stay," said Arthur. Cover us with a bow and if we get caught then at least there's a chance you can help us."

Finn nodded, stringing his bow and reaching for an arrow as Tatsushi and Arthur began creeping towards the houses. They made it to the edge of the village, to the place where they would separate to the two opposite sides of houses. That was when the silent figures of four swordsmen stepped out of the shadows and blocked their path.

# CHAPTER 5

Finn froze, watching the four swordsmen approach Arthur and Tatsushi. The plan had been not to fight unless absolutely necessary, but would Arthur and Tatsushi be able to talk their way out of this? Their odds in a fight against four grown men weren't good. He took aim at one of the men and held the bow half drawn, anxious for the situation to develop so that he knew whether to let his arrow fly. Every muscle taut, Finn waited... and waited. Nothing was happening – neither the boys nor the men were moving or making a sound. Then, as Finn's every sense strained to pick up any signal, he heard the sound of low whispering and moments later Arthur turned and began creeping back towards Finn, while Tatsushi and the four men slunk into the shadows.

"What's going on?" Finn hissed as his brother drew near.

"Those men were villagers," Arthur panted. "They're on our side. The Kurodas are holed up here alright. It seems to be the same thing as back at Tatsushi's village. They told a samurai to sacrifice his life and said they'd spare the rest."

"What about Mayuko?"

"Those four men are taking Tatsushi to the house she's in. They said they'll bust her out but they made us promise we'd help them fight the Kurodas. We had no choice," Arthur went on before Finn could react. "They said they'd raise the alarm otherwise."

Finn groaned inwardly. "How many on our side?"

"Don't know. But Tatsushi told them that they had to free Mayuko first before any fighting started."

Finn rubbed the bridge of his nose. Their mission to release Mayuko in secret and steal away before the Kurodas knew what was happening, and more importantly before Tatsushi got into a situation where he would lose his cool, wasn't panning out at all.

"There's nothing we can do about it for now,"

said Arthur pragmatically, filling Finn's silence. "We'll just have to wait for them here and then try and persuade them not to fight after all once they've freed – "

He broke off at the sound of shouts from the village, swiftly followed by the cry of a heron. Without a moment's hesitation the boys snatched up their weapons and raced forward, bows across their shoulders and swords drawn. As they reached the first house the fighting had begun already and they skidded to a stop. Halfway through the village the boys could see Tatsushi and Mayuko alongside the four swordsmen from the trees. They were arranged in two lines of three, one line facing in each direction along the road. At Tatsushi's feet lay two bodies. Beyond the group were five other men, swords drawn and snarling as they prepared to strike. Blocking Finn and Arthur's route to their friends was a second group of Kuroda's men, growing as more of them spilled out from the house in which they'd been drinking. The boys had still not been seen and Arthur thought fast.

"We need to get behind that smaller group at the far end," he whispered, and darted off the road with Finn close behind him. Arthur led the way to the back of the houses on one side of the village and the boys crept forward from house to house, sprinting each short distance where gaps between the buildings left them exposed to view from the road. They drew level with Tatsushi and his group and passed by unseen. The taunts of the Kurodas rang through the village and it seemed they were sure to attack at any moment. Praying that their enemies would have all eyes on Tatsushi's band the boys dashed to the last house and crept along its side to the road. Arthur peered around the corner of the house and ducked back again.

"We're behind them," he whispered. "I'm going to crawl across to the other side. As soon as I get there we start shooting. We should be able to get two or three of them and then Tatsushi and the others can break through whoever's left."

"Then what?"

"Then we run for it."

Finn nodded and once again notched an arrow as Arthur dropped to the floor and began crawling on his belly and elbows across the road.

The Kurodas were laughing at their enemies now, amused that a group of two children and four peasants would try and take them on. One voice in particular dominated the others – the voice belonging to the samurai who had snatched Mayuko away from her father's body the day before. Finn was trembling as the adrenalin took hold, but felt sure they would be able to get rid of the five men in front of them. And then, midway across the road, with the dust of the road surrounding him, Arthur sneezed. One of the Kurodas spun around at the sound. The man's eyes widened as he saw Arthur and

he shouted in alarm. It was to be his final breath. Barely had the sound left his lips before he crumpled to the floor, Finn's arrow protruding from between his ribs.

The whole village burst into action. Arthur leapt to his feet and whipped an arrow onto his bowstring just as Finn prepared his second shot. The four remaining Kurodas of the nearest group leapt to either side of the road, seeking cover behind the houses. Two of them fell as they ran, Finn and Arthur both finding their marks. The larger mob of Kurodas at the other end of the village bellowed in rage and began running towards them, brandishing swords and spears, while Tatsushi, Mayuko and the villagers, seeing their opportunity, exploded into a sprint along the road towards Finn, Arthur and the darkness that engulfed the road beyond the edge of the village.

Spears hissed into the ground around them and they ran for their lives. As their feet pounded the ground beneath them they left the village behind and darkness swallowed them up.

"We should get off the road!" Finn panted.

"Impossible for now," someone replied – "There are high rocks on both sides. We will be past them soon." They heard the neighing of horses behind them and each of them tried to squeeze a little more speed out of their burning muscles. And then they heard more horses in front of them and they skidded to a halt. It was only a second before they saw what lay ahead, but the moment seemed to stretch impossibly as their hearts sank to new lows.

"Kuroda's men are on a rampage," Tatsushi shouted desperately at the shadowy figures of several horsemen who had begun to take form before their eyes. "Whoever you are please let us past!"

"Hanzo Uchida's son," came a familiar voice. "Let them through."

"Ryu!" cried Mayuko, and the boys could have wept with relief.

"And seven loyal samurai," Ryu replied.

"The Kurodas are too many," Tatsushi began. But his voice was nearly drowned out by the roar of the onrushing gang.

"Forward, stay mounted," someone shouted.

The seven samurai kicked their horses on, and the men from the village turned and followed them while Ryu wheeled his horse around, blocking the remaining group.

"We should stay and fight," Tatsushi protested.

"No," Ryu snapped. "Stay focussed. You came for Mayuko and now she is free. We run now and plan our next move against Kuroda himself."

"He's right," said Finn.

Tatsushi argued no further and the group pressed forward away from the village just as the shouts and screams of battle began to echo between the rocks behind them.

EXTRACT FROM *WARRIOR HEROES*
BY FINN BLADE

## ORDINARY LIFE IN MEDIEVAL JAPAN

Different types of people are ranked in a strict order in medieval Japan. This is OK if you are near the top of the ranking system, but not so good if you are low down.

## LORD

Right at the top of the pile is the Lord or Daimyo. He owns most of the land in the area, lives in a fancy palace and has plenty of servants and an army of samurai to do his bidding.

## SAMURAI

They are the warriors who fight for the Lord, so they are respected and feared and many of them become very wealthy (despite their code of honour saying that they should live simply).

Nobody of a lower rank is allowed to carry a sword, so you're safe from jealous commoners.

## COMMONERS

Farmers, then craftsmen, then merchants - in that order - make up the ranks of commoners. They are not allowed to use a family name, they pay taxes to the Lord and are generally not able to do much about it, unless they have a particularly good Lord.

## OUTCASTS

The lowest of the low, outcasts are tasked with the dirty jobs like executing criminals, butchering animals for food, sorting out the sewage etc. If your parents are outcasts then so are you and you can't change that. End of story.

# CHAPTER 6

Ryu looked on impassively as his four young companions gulped water from a stream and tore greedily through the food that he handed around. They had left the road behind them a couple of hours previously and had scrambled uphill along a rough trail until the trees and air had grown markedly thinner. At Ryu's insistence they had marched in total silence in case they were being followed, and after their experiences with the Kurodas over the past twenty-four hours, nobody had disagreed with him. Not that they would have been able to say much while they walked in any case – the climb uphill on top of everything else they had endured so far had been utterly exhausting. Ryu had abandoned his horse on the road and marched with them on foot. He seemed impossibly fit for an old man, and it was he who first found the strength to speak.

"Another hour's walk will bring us to a temple where they will give us shelter I am sure."

"And the Kurodas?" Arthur asked through a mouthful of rice. "When will we know whether they have followed us? When will we know who won the battle?"

"The seven men who rode with me to your aid are very skilled warriors, but even with help from the villagers they would have been outnumbered by the Kurodas – and they too know how to fight. My guess is that there won't be many left on either side, regardless of who wins the battle."

Mayuko lowered her head. "All that death because of me..." she murmured.

"No!" Tatsushi shook his head forcefully. "They brought it on themselves. They killed our father and kidnapped you."

"Thank you," Mayuko put out a hand and Tatsushi took hold of it protectively. "But now that I have been rescued we must do something to protect our village. I overheard the Kurodas saying that they have seized Castle Kuruyama."

"As soon as we have rested that is where we are going," said Tatsushi, the fire back in his eyes. "And there we will kill Kenji Kuroda." Mayuko's pale face was completely expressionless as she nodded her understanding.

"But for now," said Ryu, getting to his feet. "We are one more hour away from the temple I mentioned, where we will find food and rest, and possibly a new ally."

Everyone's ears pricked up at this but Ryu would say no more and began to lead on up the trail in the moonlight with the others strung out in a short line behind him. Talking stopped once more as their muscles began straining, and the only sounds were the panting of the climbers, the clack and crunch of stones underfoot, and the occasional scurrying of a frightened animal.

After what seemed like an age they broke through the tree line and saw before them the shadow of a mountain's peak, silhouetted against a sky tinged with the faintest hint of dawn. Finn and Arthur both felt light-headed, the thin air and their exhaustion combining to create a woozy, drowsy feeling as if they had stayed too long in a very hot bath. It was strange to feel so comfortable at the tail end of such a long ordeal, and it was in this state that they followed the trail around a buttress of rock and first caught sight of the temple they were headed for, perched on a wide ledge above the trail.

Like all the others they had seen this was an elegant wooden building, though unlike the others this had clearly been dragged bit by bit up the side of the mountain. There was nothing imposing about it, but the elegant, swooping curve of the roof, the large, perfectly spaced wooden pillars that supported it and the muted reds and greens with which it was painted were so pleasing to the eye that even Arthur, not normally one to appreciate the style of a building, was clearly impressed.

The five of them continued along the last stretch of the trail that led to a wide flight of steps in front of the temple and as they approached they heard the chanting of deep, bass voices that reverberated solemnly inside.

"Monks," Finn whispered. "They get up early."

As they mounted the steps they were met by a shaven-headed man draped in a long, yellow robe. Ryu explained that he was seeking shelter for his young companions and that he wished to speak with the abbot. The monk smiled and bowed to each of them in turn. Finn and Arthur were getting used to bowing, and responded in kind before the monk led them through the temple gate to a large, raised trough of water. Watching closely to see what the others did and following their example, the boys took some of the water into their mouths and spat it out again at their feet, before rubbing water across their foreheads. These unknown rituals complete, the man led them silently past rows of chanting monks, across a small courtyard and to a room with several sleeping mats rolled up on the floor.

"Sleep," he said kindly. "You have had a long journey. When you wake we will talk."

For the first time since the adventure had

begun, the boys felt safe and judging by the slumped shoulders of Mayuko and Tatsushi they felt the same. Each of them unrolled a mat, collapsed onto it and pulled a blanket over themselves.

Only Ryu gave any indication that he could resist the urge to sleep. Finn yawned and was already closing his eyes as Tatsushi asked the question that had been on all their minds.

"Who is the ally that you hoped we might find in the monastery?"

Ryu looked at him and smiled. "You will succeed even without his help Tatsushi. But he would be the perfect guide. Some call him the vanishing one."

"Akira!" Tatsushi exclaimed, and both Finn and Arthur felt a surge of excitement at the thought that they might meet the vanishing samurai from Tatsushi's story.

"I will say no more. For now you must sleep. You are safe, Mayuko is safe, your friends are safe and you have all done very well. Tomorrow begins tomorrow."

Even the thought of the vanishing samurai was not enough to keep them awake. Their aching limbs relaxed for the first time in an age, and in seconds the four young adventurers were asleep.

# CHAPTER 7

Finn woke slowly. The room was hot, and through its small window he could see that the sun was high in the sky. He sat up and stretched, aching in every part of his body, as he looked around the room. Ryu was missing, but the other three lay sleeping. It felt as though his body weighed twice as much as it had the day before, and with some considerable effort

Finn rose and wandered through the drapes that hung in place of a door and out into the courtyard.

The monk who had welcomed them in at dawn sat cross-legged under the shade of a parasol.

"Do you feel rested?" he asked gently, looking up as Finn approached him.

Finn nodded half-heartedly and the man laughed.

"You will soon feel better," he said. "Ryu has been telling me about your adventures. You have all been very brave." Finn yawned, and the monk turned back to face the open space of the courtyard, watching as a monkey scampered across the ground.

"You are friends of William Blade, I understand," said the monk quietly, still watching the monkey. "And again the Kurodas try to seize what is not theirs to take. These truly are strange times."

"Did you know him as well?" Finn asked, suddenly wary.

Before the monk had time to reply Ryu emerged from the temple across the courtyard, deep in conversation with another monk, and as the two men approached Ryu caught Finn's eye and pursed his lips.

"We need to press on," he said curtly and entered the room where the others slept. Finn looked at the two monks but their faces gave nothing away. He was beginning to realise that the medieval Japanese did not express their emotions as readily as people back home and he felt strangely awkward all of a sudden. He was relieved when the others emerged from the room, yawning and blinking in the bright mountain sunlight.

"I have spoken with the abbot and he has offered us much that will help," said Ryu, following the group out of the room. "Provisions and horses also."

"And Akira?" Arthur enquired. The monk standing beside Ryu shook his head.

"We do not know anyone by that name," he said. Then, nodding at the friendly monk under the parasol he continued, "but we can offer you a guide to help you across the pass and down into the valley where you will find Castle Kuruyama." Curiosity flickered at the back of Finn's mind and then vanished.

"You are very kind sir," said Ryu, bowing as

the others tried to hide their disappointment that they would not be travelling with the great vanishing warrior. "If we succeed in our endeavours we will see to it that your monastery receives a reward."

"We seek no reward. If Kuroda can be stopped then that is reward enough."

Ryu bowed again, then set about herding the others back into the room where they gathered their belongings and weapons and then followed Ryu back through the temple and out onto the steps that lead down to the trail. Their friendly monk came with them, carrying a long staff and a sack full of food.

"What is your name, sir?" Tatsushi asked the monk as they each mounted one of the six horses that were waiting for them.

"I have no name," came the reply. "I renounced it when I joined the monastery." Again Finn felt a flicker of curiosity but before he could explore it Ryu was barking out instructions again.

"We follow the monk and we do not stop until we are through the pass and back down below the tree line. Now that the Kurodas know they are meeting with some resistance we do not have long before they unleash their fury on the villages."

They bowed to the abbot who stood at the temple gate and then set off along the mountain trail. To Finn and Arthur the ride was horribly uncomfortable. The horses walked or trotted along the trail, shaking them like bags of bones on top of thinly quilted saddles that offered little comfort. Looking ahead Finn saw how much better their Japanese friends were as riders. The monk in particular was impressive. With his long staff in one hand, reins in the other, and his back perfectly straight he seemed almost as though he were leading some graceful royal procession.

The scenery was beautiful too. A sweep of scree tumbled down the side of the mountain to the left before being swallowed up by the trees they had climbed through, while beyond the forest the ocean glittered in the sunlight. Before long the view was lost. They had reached the pass and were crossing a ridge in between two peaks, the trail snaking out in front of them down the other side of the mountain and into a deep valley, bordered on either side by long spurs of rock.

They reached the tree line after a couple more uncomfortable hours, and heaving sighs of relief

Finn and Arthur slid off their mounts to join the others sitting on the trunk of a fallen tree. They were just beginning to enjoy some much-needed refreshment when Ryu sat bolt upright. His eyes rolled up in his head and he fell forward to reveal the shaft of an arrow thrusting up from his back.

With cries of mixed rage and anguish, Tatsushi and Mayuko leapt up as more arrows hissed through the air.

"On your horses and back up the trail," said the monk calmly but firmly, and they followed his instructions, leaping into their saddles and hunching down behind their horses' heads. Arthur was in the lead, and as he reached a huge boulder he took cover behind it and dismounted once more before scrambling up the side of the boulder to peer over the top, with Finn not far behind him.

The monk had not moved. He stood calmly by the fallen tree as three menacing men on horseback circled him. With a sick feeling Finn

recognised the man who had kidnapped Mayuko. His first thought was for Tatsushi. What would he do if he recognised the man? Looking back down to the bottom of the boulder he saw Tatsushi and Mayuko still mounted and with anger flashing in their eyes as they prepared to charge back down the trail.

Arthur already had his bow strung and Finn scrambled to do the same. For the second time they both took aim at Kuroda's men, but just as they were about to shoot something extraordinary happened before their eyes. The monk looked straight at the boys and held their gaze. Then in a flash of impossibly quick motion he crouched down, grabbed the end of his staff and drove the other end up in the air to connect with one of the horsemen's faces. Never once looking away from the boys he gave two more swift thrusts and all three men toppled to the ground.

It was the most explosive, skilful display of close combat that either of them had ever seen, and they lowered their bows, both of them trembling with shock. Judging by the look on Mayuko and Tatsushi's faces they were equally taken aback while the monk, still gazing up calmly, beckoned them down the trail.

## THE WAY OF THE WARRIOR

Bushido, or the way of the warrior, was the code of honour by which samurai were supposed to live. A bit like chivalry for knights in Europe, the idea was that this code would encourage these highly trained warriors to behave with nobility and fairness. Needless to say, it didn't always work out that way. Here are some of the things that samurai were expected to show:

## COURAGE

This is so you set a good example to the rest of the population (or so you will win battles when your Lord needs you to).

## FRUGALITY

Living simply and not getting too comfortable so that you can focus on strengthening your character (or so that you never get above yourself and try to steal land or wealth from your Lord).

## CHARITY

This is so you don't act with cruelty to the peasants beneath you (and so the peasants don't get too annoyed and start a revolution).

## LOYALTY

Because it's good to be loyal, and it's especially good for your Lord if you are loyal as this prevents you from trying to overthrow him.

## HONOUR

Because if your reputation really matters to you then your Lord can easily bring you down by finding some way to disgrace you.

Clearly those are all admirable qualities. Maybe the way of the warrior really was just about being the best person you could be, not just about Japanese rulers trying to control everything. You decide!

# CHAPTER 8

"We should kill them where they lie," Tatsushi snarled, standing over the unconscious bodies of the Kuroda men with his sword raised. The group had clambered back down to join the monk.

"We should not," replied the monk quietly.

"You have to say that, you're a monk. But they killed my father, they took Mayuko, they tried to kill us and now they have killed Ryu." Tears rolled down Tatsushi's cheeks at this latest, cruel loss.

"Tatsushi," Finn began tentatively. "We should only kill them if it will help us achieve what we are here for."

"And are we not in part here for revenge?" Tatsushi implored, though he lowered his sword.

"You may desire revenge but you must never act on it," said the monk. "If you do then you are little better than these men, and you will certainly fail to bring down Kenji Kuroda. I know better than most what lies ahead and you should believe me when I say you cannot succeed in such a dangerous venture unless your mind is free to focus perfectly."

Finn frowned.

"What do you mean you know what lies ahead?"

"I know what it is to fight. And I know Castle Kuruyama. The abbot chose me as your guide for good reason."

"But these men..." Tatsushi choked on the words and the monk held up his hand.

"Remember why you are here. A great many people will suffer if you do not succeed in stopping Kuroda. Anything else, be it curiosity, anger, pain, hate, pride – anything else is a distraction. Your father must have taught you that. We have very little time now before Kuroda will strike properly at the villages and we must hurry. These men here will not wake until tomorrow – I have some knowledge of these things."

"Some knowledge," Finn snorted, "The way you brought those men down – I've never seen such skill!"

"Finn's right." Tatsushi was staring hard at the monk. "I have never seen anything like it either. I've only ever heard of one living man who had truly mastered the art of combat. But you couldn't be him... You're not... not..."

"Akira?" Mayuko finished.

"I have no name," replied the monk. "And we have no time." He lifted Ryu's body and carefully draped it across the back of one of the horses, tying it down. "The horse will find his way back to the monastery," he explained.

Mayuko and her brother whispered their goodbye's to Ryu's motionless body and then slapped the horse's flank to send him on his way.

The horse trotted up the trail as the four friends and the monk mounted their horses again and began their descent through the thickening forest. They were in the shadow of the mountain again so could not see the sun but judging by the colour of the sky, sunset was approaching as the trail widened out into a rough road and they were able to ride alongside one another. The monk had said they would be in view of the castle by nightfall and sure enough as the road reached the extreme of one of the mountain's spurs and turned out of the valley into a broad plain, Finn and Arthur were treated to their first sight of Castle Kuruyama.

Smooth, grey stone walls curved forbiddingly out of the ground atop an isolated hill in the middle of a vast plain. The stone walls lead to

the brilliant white upper part of the castle which was topped with layer upon layer of curved roof as if no sooner had one roof been completed than another storey had been added, and another roof. The building looked like something from a weird fairy tale – beautiful, fantastical, and utterly impenetrable.

"How do we get inside that?" Arthur breathed.

"And how do we get out alive?" Finn added.

"I know the way," the monk replied, calmly. "We wait for nightfall and we climb the walls – to the top. That is where Kuroda will be. If we try to enter the castle through any of the windows lower down we will have to fight our way up and he will know we are coming."

"It doesn't look possible," said Tatsushi doubtfully.

"But it is. I have done it before. Many years ago Lord Kuruyama asked me to show him how I would enter the castle if I were his assassin so that he could improve his defences."

"You really are Akira, aren't you?" Tatsushi tried to contain his excitement. "You fought alongside my father."

"And alongside William Blade," Finn commented.

"And alongside Lord Kuruyama and a great many others," the monk replied, finally dropping the pretence. "When the war with the Kurodas was over I vowed that I would never again serve as a samurai. I vanished from the world and sought refuge in the mountains. I always knew though that one day my skills would be needed again, and now here we are…"

Akira laid out his plan. They would send the horses back up the mountain and wait for nightfall. The large village that sprawled out to one side of the castle would be carefully watched by Kuroda's men, so they would approach the castle from the opposite side. Akira would lead them to the top storey of the castle where they would lie hidden for an hour. During this time Akira would venture into the village and find the many men who he knew would want to avenge Lord Kuruyama's death and might be persuaded to rise up once Kuroda was dead himself. When he returned they would enter the castle through a hidden opening in the roof designed as an escape hatch, and challenge Kuroda. It was an audacious plan and there seemed to be many things that could thwart them, but the stakes were high and they knew that there was no turning back now that they had already challenged Kuroda's authority. Akira's experience and quiet authority, not to mention his status as a living legend was so powerful that following his lead seemed their best chance of success, and nobody disagreed with him. Akira sat down under a tree, motioned to the others to do the same, and handed round some food and water as they settled in to wait for nightfall.

* * *

Not until the plain was in total darkness did Akira signal that it was time to move on, instructing Finn and Arthur to walk the horses a short way back towards the mountain and send them home. As they set off into the darkness Finn was grateful for the rare opportunity to speak with Arthur alone. They had been by Tatsushi's side almost constantly since their arrival from the ocean, and Finn wanted to agree their strategy.

"Everyone keeps saying that Tatsushi must not look for revenge," he said in a low voice as they led the horses along the road. "And that's what Hanzo Uchida's ghost said back at the museum too."

Arthur nodded. "But Kuroda does have to be killed because otherwise the village will be destroyed in any case, which is what Hanzo Uchida wanted us to prevent."

"OK, so there are only two things that matter," said Finn, tugging at the bridle of a horse that had paused to graze. "Kuroda must die, but Tatsushi must stay in control of his anger. At least Akira seems to agree. He doesn't seem that keen on killing but we've seen what he can do. One of us will kill Kuroda and we just have to trust that Akira can take care of the rest and get us all out alive. Any sign of Tatsushi losing it and we have to step in.

Other than that, we'll just have to see what we find when we get to the castle."

Arthur agreed, and after sending the horses on their way they were soon back with the others and taking their first nervous steps towards Castle Kuruyama.

EXTRACT FROM *WARRIOR HEROES*
BY FINN BLADE

## JAPANESE CASTLES

The Japanese really love their castles. At one time there were over 5,000 of them dotted around the country, many of them perched high up in the mountains. A castle can be anything from a small wooden fortress to a major defended palace but of course they all have one thing in common. They are there so that the people inside them can defeat whoever might try to attack.

The classic Japanese castle, is built on a mound or hill with a stone base and a series of wooden towers or keeps above. Just like European castles, they are full

of cunning ways to kill whoever
is trying to get in. Some of the
cleverest are:

- Arranging long wooden spikes in
  the moat.

- Pouring hot sand out of windows
  onto your attackers.

- Shooting arrows through slits in
  the walls that are so narrow you
  will never get hit yourself.

- Trapdoors in the floor that open
  up onto lethal drops if you don't
  know where you're walking.

- Hanging tree trunks from beams
  so that you can drop them on your
  attackers' heads.

- The nightingale floor makes it
  impossible to walk across the
  floor inside a castle tower

without making a noise. Iron nails in the floorboards and joists are positioned so that they rub together and chirp like a bird whenever someone stands on that part of the floor. Like an alarm, but much easier on the ear!

All this said it is actually quite unusual for an army to attack a castle and try to gain entry in Japan. Mostly castles are strongholds in which Lords could rule, safely out of reach of everyone else. Their biggest threats come from assassins rather than armies, and castle builders thought up lots of defences against assassins too.

# CHAPTER 9

A sliver of moon provided just enough light for each member of the group to follow the person in front of them, and Akira led the way along an easy path that followed the riverbank. Ahead they could still make out the swoop of the castle's many roofs, and to its right they could see the lights of the village. When they were about a mile away Akira led them away from the river to avoid any unwanted encounters closer to the castle, and they skirted around in a wide arc to the left, picking their way more carefully along the banks that framed a patchwork of watery rice fields. It was slow work, and by the time they had put the castle between themselves and the village Finn and Arthur were both panting and sweating, despite the level ground. They still had a mile to go as they had been circling the castle, and Akira allowed them a few moments' rest as he went over his plan one last time and provided some final details.

"As we draw near the castle we will meet the river again – it forms the moat on this side and there are no guard posts. From the moment we cross the river we proceed in total silence.

You should imagine at all times that you are right outside an open window to a room full of armed men who want to kill you. Not even your breathing should be heard. I will climb each stage first then lower a rope and each of you will follow in turn. When we are on top of the final roof I will lead you to the hatch and there you will wait, on the roof, until I return.

"Two more things," he went on. "First, should anything happen to me and I do not return you should know that the top level of the castle has a nightingale floor."

"What does that mean?" asked Arthur.

"The floorboards are laid with nails that rub against one another to squeak when you walk on them," said Finn. "It makes it very difficult to creep up on anyone."

Akira nodded at Finn and continued, "The second thing is even more important. Arthur, Finn, Mayuko, you must watch Tatsushi carefully. If it appears that he is going to be consumed by anger then you must make sure that it is not he who kills Kuroda. Even if he succeeds, if he kills in anger then nothing good will come of this as you will win little support afterwards. Mayuko, boys, will you ensure that Kuroda is not killed in anger?"

Three voices replied that they would.

"Then it is time," said Akira, leading them forward once more.

* * *

Twenty minutes later they were crouched nervously at the foot of the castle as Akira uncoiled a length of rope and showed them how to sling their swords across their backs in a way that would leave them free to climb. They had not seen any guards, nor had they been seen – Akira's plan so far had been flawless and his followers trusted him completely, but staring up at the looming castle above with its overhanging roofs and smooth walls sent a shiver of fear through Finn's body. The climb itself looked terrifying, and the idea of the brutal warlord awaiting them at the top was more terrifying still.

Akira tucked his monk's robes up around his legs, squeezed each of the group's arms in turn, and began the first stage of his stealthy ascent. He moved smoothly and silently up the slope of the castle's stone base, pausing for a moment when he reached the foot of the first vertical white wall. He had started at a corner of the sloping base, and the corner ridge formed by the stones had seemed easy enough to ascend. But the vertical white walls looked unclimbable. Akira stood at the bottom of the sheer walls and inched away from the corner, first one way then the other, listening carefully for any sounds of disturbance within. He reached up and put his hands one above the other in one of the tiny arrow slits that punctuated the smoothness of the walls, and then began walking his feet up until he was hanging in a crouching position, then placed a toe in the arrow slit and walked his hands up to the top of the slit. The first roof was at least five feet above his head as he stared up and began to bounce up and down on his toe-hold, before launching into an explosive leap. He shot up the wall, his body now fully extended, and caught hold of the upturned lip of the first roof. His feet swung out into space, then silently connected with the wall once more and he was able to scramble up and onto the roof. Moments later the rope snaked down the wall until the end grazed the stones a short way above Mayuko's head.

Showing no evidence of fear, Mayuko then climbed up to the rope, and from there proceeded to walk her feet up the wall, and her hands up the rope until she was able to take hold of Akira's outstretched arm and join him on the edge of the first roof. The three boys followed suit and the first stage of the climb was complete. They repeated the process and had

begun to settle into a routine by the time they reached the third stage. Although the climb was horribly precarious, Finn found that if he just concentrated on the next few steps it somehow felt possible. He was the last of the group to climb the third stage, and he was half way up the rope when a man's head emerged from a window a few feet to his right.

Finn froze. The man seemed to be alone. There were no voices coming from the window and he was gazing lazily into the distance. Finn willed the man to go away. His arms, already exhausted from the climbing, were beginning to burn with the strain and his hands were sweating meaning that he had to grip the rope tighter still to avoid slipping. He looked up at the roof above, praying that one of the others would see the predicament he was in. For several agonising seconds that seemed like minutes, nothing happened. Finn tried desperately to think of a way of getting to the man and dealing with him without drawing the attention of anyone else inside, but he couldn't. Even if he managed to get to the man his hands would be on the rope and he would be completely defenceless. But his hands were going to give out soon and he had to get to safety. Very slowly he began inching his way sideways across the wall, away from the window and around the corner of the castle onto the next wall before lowering himself silently back to the roof below.

Just as his feet touched the roof and his legs took the weight off his hands, Akira's head appeared over the lip of the roof above. The monk acted without hesitation. He swung himself back down onto the wall, holding his full weight from the roof with one arm. With his free hand he brought his staff down off the roof and jabbed the tip down. It connected with the base of the man's neck, and the immediate danger was over. The man slumped forward and lay unconscious, head and shoulders still protruding from the window. Akira untied the climbing rope and climbed down to sit on the window ledge. He looped the rope under the man's arms, hoisted his unconscious weight out of the window and lowered him slowly to the ground before retrieving the rope.

By the time Akira had climbed back up and reset the rope Finn felt he had just enough strength in his hands to make the climb again and he wasted no time, praying as he climbed that Akira's skills were as honed as they seemed, and that the man would not wake up too soon. As he reached the next roof and joined the others he slumped down, gasping and trembling. His concerned friends gathered round but Akira shook his head, placed his finger to his lips, and began the next stage of the climb.

Finn could not bring his nerves under control, and although the remaining two stages of the climb were covered without incident, by the time he pulled himself up onto the top roof of the main tower his knees were literally knocking together. Tatsushi held his arm and helped him sit, while Akira tied the rope to two points to create a rail the others could hold on to while he was gone. Leaving Tatsushi and Finn, the monk guided Mayuko and Arthur along the rail and showed them the location of the roof hatch before they regrouped next to Finn.

*"One hour,"* Akira mouthed. And then he disappeared back over the lip of the roof and was gone, leaving Tatsushi, Mayuko and the boys

alone in the night on the roof of Castle Kuruyama. They waited, each lost in their thoughts, none moving or making a sound. None of them could have said how long the monk had been gone when suddenly the roof hatch opened and the first armoured guard climbed up onto the roof, shouted down into the castle and grinned at the would-be assassins.

# CHAPTER 10

Tatsushi had his sword drawn before the others had even moved, and he sprinted across the roof towards the guard, parrying the man's vicious spear-thrust and charging into his chest. The guard stumbled backwards, tripped on the roof hatch and with a terrified shriek, toppled sideways over the edge of the castle. A series of crashing sounds marked his broken fall from roof to roof as Tatsuhi flipped the hatch closed again.

"Finn, your bow!" Tatsuhsi shouted, but Finn was ahead of him. Now that the action had started there was no space for nerves, and Finn already had his bow strung and an arrow notched and ready.

"If that hatch is the only way up onto the roof then we can hold them," said Arthur with confidence. "They can only climb up one at a time. Finn, shoot anyone who puts their head up. The rest of us need to find another way of getting to Kuroda."

*"Akira!"* Tatsushi cried in desperation, and for a few moments they each listened for some sign that the vanishing samurai was coming to their rescue.

And then the door of the hatch opened

again. A man shot up through it, slicing a circle in the air with his sword as he did so, before planting his feet on either side of the hatch. Finn's arrow was lodged in his chest before he could move any further.

"They're children," he croaked, and fell back through the roof. Below them they heard the sound of many running feet, urgent, hushed debate, and the chirping of the nightingale floor. Then, total silence.

"What are they doing?" Finn whispered, and then a voice boomed up at them, roaring out the question in a raging crescendo.

*"Who sent you?"*

"Kenji Kuroda sent us," Tatsushi called back.

*"Liar! I am Kenji Kuroda. Do I send assassins to take my own life?"*

"My name is Tatsushi Uchida! You sent me the day your men killed my father. Your men kidnapped my sister. Your men have been going from village to village killing and stealing like a gang of criminals and I challenge you, if you have any honour in your black, diseased blood you will come up here and fight like a true warrior!"

"I am your Lord," Kuroda shouted back. "I will not dirty my hands fighting a traitor and an assassin."

"Kuruyama was my lord," Tatsushi replied. "You are nothing but a thief and a murderer. As the son of a samurai who served our rightful Lord, in the name of Kuruyama and all who are loyal to him still I claim this castle. I have as much right to call myself Lord as you do."

There was a long silence. Finn kept an arrow trained on the space above the hatch.

"If he does come up," Tatsushi whispered, "You let me fight him properly. The only way this can end well is if he accepts the challenge and loses."

Finn looked over at Mayuko and Arthur, who both nodded.

"Tatsushi Uchida!" Kuroda yelled. "I accept your challenge. But we will fight inside the castle."

"No!" Tatsushi shouted back. "Your men will kill us as soon as we set one foot inside. Up here, where the odds are even."

Another silence, then Kuroda's cruel voice snarled a reply. "On the roof then. It makes no difference where I kill you. Tell me how many you are and I will bring the same number of witnesses."

"Five," Tatsushi called back, before realising his mistake. Akira was not with them.

"Very well," Kuroda growled. "Four of my men are coming up and I will follow."

A few seconds later the hatch opened again and a murderous-looking man thrust his head and shoulders through the hole. Finn kept his arrow trained on the man as he climbed up.

"Over there," called Arthur, pointing the man to the far side of the roof. Three more men followed after, each heavily armed but none with weapons drawn.

Still Finn kept his arrow trained on the hatchway, and now Kuroda himself emerged.

He was a huge barrel-chested tree trunk of a man and Finn's heart sank. Kuroda looked up at him and bared his teeth.

"Put the bow down, boy. Where is this Uchida?"

Finn angled his head in Tatsushi's direction and lowered the bow. Kuroda sprang up onto the roof and turned to face his challenger.

"So your father was Hanzo Uchida," the huge man spat the name. "He fought with Kuruyama against my father. I will enjoy wiping out his line tonight. Tell me," he went on with a cruel smile. "Did they give him a good death?" Too late Finn saw the rage flash in Tatsushi's eyes.

"I will have my revenge!" Tatsushi screamed.

"No Tatsushi!" Mayuko cried, but already Tatsushi was lost in his hate. Kuroda smirked and his sword flashed as he drew it and stepped up onto the top ridge of the roof to face Tatsushi, who was poised at the other end.

"Tatsushi!" someone shouted, and Finn gasped with relief at the unmistakable sound of Akira's voice. "Remember what is at stake. Your desire for revenge is too strong. You cannot focus. You cannot win the fight."

Akira stepped up into view from the other side of the roof, pushing up on his staff and standing in front of Tatsushi.

"And who are you?" Kuroda snarled as Akira put his hand on Tatsushi's sword and lowered it.

"A monk," he replied. "I have no name."

"The boy challenged me, monk, and he will pay with his life."

Akira smiled and bowed to Kuroda. "But as you can see," he said, "now you are also being challenged by a monk." Kuroda's men reached for their swords.

Finn snatched up his bow and took aim. "The first man to draw dies," he said calmly, and the men stayed where they were.

Kuroda howled, and raising his sword over his head he ran along the ridge towards the monk. Akira planted his feet a short way apart and brought his staff up so that he held it horizontally at chest level, arms thrust forward. Kuroda came to within a few steps of Akira and then leapt up in the air, slashing down as he flew forwards. In one fluid movement Akira crouched, twisted his staff to vertical and thrust powerfully upwards into Kuroda's

chest. The warlord grunted, his eyes wide with shock as he was propelled backwards through the air, and with a final roar of rage, soared over the edge of the roof and down into the darkness below. There was no series of bumps and crashes this time, just a long scream and a few seconds later a dull thud as he hit the ground, far below.

Tatsushi slumped to his knees, tears once

again streaming down his cheeks as he gazed up at Akira in silent thanks. The monk touched him lightly on the forehead.

"We still have work to do," he said. "Finn, be sure that those men don't move while I share the good news with the village." He climbed back over the edge of the roof from which he had emerged only moments ago and reappeared with a large red lantern, which he proceeded to light and hang from the end of the roof ridge. In its warm red glow Kuroda's guards looked even more shocked than Finn and Arthur felt. A great cheer could be heard from below, and everyone turned to look down at a swarm of moving lights in the village. It took Finn a few moments to figure out what he was looking at.

"The villagers!" he exclaimed. "They're coming to the castle."

"That is correct," said Akira, turning to Kuroda's men. "I have a message for you to take to your brothers in arms inside the castle. Your lord is dead. The villagers are armed with a supply of weapons that Lord Kuruyama, in his wisdom, kept hidden in a pit beyond the village. There are over one hundred of them and in five minutes they will be at the castle gates. Soon word will spread and by dawn they will be joined by the men of all the villages that have suffered at Kuroda's hand. You will be surrounded, and outnumbered, by an army of people whom you have wronged.

"You have one chance, and one chance only, to leave this place with honour and with your lives.

That moment is now. I suggest you act quickly."

Ashen-faced, Kuroda's men dashed to the hatch and relayed the message. Within two minutes the castle gates were open and men were streaming out of it and scattering themselves across the plain.

Just as the gates opened, Finn and Arthur both shivered. Something in the air pressure had changed and grown closer. A gust of wind shook them where they stood on the roof and looking up they saw that the stars and moon were now hidden.

"We should go inside," said Akira. "The top storey will be empty now."

"Do you mind if Finn and I stay on the roof for a few minutes?" Arthur asked. Akira looked at him strangely, then smiled and ushered Tatsushi and Mayuko down through the hatch.

"Do give my regards to William Blade," said Akira, and then he too was gone.

"I think we're done," said Finn, and Arthur nodded.

"I just can't believe the Professor never told us that he used to be like us..."

But before he could say more the rain began, and just as it had on the day that they arrived it seemed to fill every bit of space until it felt as though the castle were underwater and they were kicking up towards the surface. The watery world began to spin around them, faster and faster, until the castle, the weapons and all evidence of their adventure had blurred into nothing.

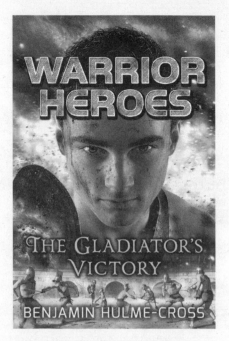

# WARRIOR HEROES
## The Gladiator's Victory

### Benjamin Hulme-Cross

Trapped in their great grandfather's museum,
brothers Arthur and Finn must help the terrifying
ghosts of warriors find peace. Will the boys be able
to convince a fearsome Gladiator to fight for his
freedom? Even if they do, will they be able to escape
the clutches of a powerful Roman senator?

£4.99

9781472904652

Extract from
# WARRIOR HEROES
# The Gladiator's Victory

"You're going to get a beating boy! I said stand up!" Arthur heard the words as if he were listening through a thick wall. As he slowly opened his eyes and began to take in his surroundings, he became sharply aware of a terrible stench filling his nostrils. Looking up, he saw that he was lying in a narrow alleyway, hemmed in by tall buildings on either side. The stench, he soon realised, came from the mounds of rotting food and sewage that muddied the ground.

"Where am I?" Arthur groaned to nobody, pushing himself up on his elbow and blinking up at a dusty, orange sky.

"You're on my patch, boy," a harsh voice replied, and Arthur twisted round slowly to see a rough, scarred, street-wise looking teenager glaring down at him, slapping the end of what seemed to be a well-used club into the palm of his hand. "I'm Festus. And that's all you need to know. Now get up and tell me why you're here or by Jupiter I'll crush your skull before you say another word."

Suddenly, Arthur didn't feel so blurry eyed. He dragged himself quickly to his feet and held his hands up, noticing for the first time that a gang of similarly menacing boys stood behind Festus.

"I... I'm new here. I don't know where I am," Arthur spluttered, still slightly confused and trying to buy time. He held out little hope of out-fighting or out-running the gang.

"You're on my patch, boy," Festus repeated with a sneer. "This is Rome. Welcome to the greatest city in the world," he added sarcastically.

"Eh... Thanks," said Arthur, stepping forward warily. "Now if you'll just let me past I'll be on my way and get off your patch."

Festus stood motionless. "What do you think lads?"

"Let's teach him a lesson," one of the gang called back, and the rest began cheering. Arthur's heart sank. He quickly tried to think of a way out of this situation. Only one idea came to mind and it was risky, but he had to find a way out of this mess. Taking a deep breath and puffing out his chest, he glared at the gang...

*About the author*

Growing up in London I spent a lot of time sitting on the Underground, daydreaming and reading books. Historical adventures in far-flung lands were always my favourite and I used to love visiting castles and ruins.

After I left home I lived in Japan for a while and learned all about the Samurai. Now I've swapped the city for the countryside, and as well as reading books I also write stories and plays for young people.

The thing I like most about being a writer is playing around with ideas for stories in my head, which is daydreaming really so not much has changed!